# Rainy's Powwow

*written by* Linda Theresa Raczek

*illustrated by* Gary Bennett

rising moon

*Books for Young Readers from Northland Publishing*

The illustrations were done in gouache on watercolor paper
The text type was set in Golden Cockerel
The display type was set in Formal
Composed in the United States of America
Designed by Jennifer Schaber
Edited by Aimee Jackson
Production Supervised by Lisa Brownfield

Printed in China by Palace Press International

FIRST IMPRESSION
ISBN 0-87358-686-7

Library of Congress Catalog Card Number pending

0643/5M/6-99

To my mother and father.
—L. T. R.

To Madeline, Angie, and Nick.
—G. B.

The Thunderbird Powwow was about to begin. Lorraine and her little brother, Raymond, waited patiently in the cool shade of the dance arbor. Beside them, hunched over her cane, sat the very old woman they called Grandmother White Hair.

The old woman nudged Lorraine and pointed to the window of blue sky overhead. A lone eagle circled on silent wings.

"Even our Uncle, the Eagle, honors us with his circle dance today," she said, chuckling.

Suddenly the arbor shook with drumbeats and the high voices of the singers. The people stood to show their respect for the dancers who were lined up for the Grand Entry.

The old woman touched Lorraine's arm. "Will you stand for me, children?" Lorraine looked at Grandmother's cane cradled in her old hands. She saw how small and frail Grandmother was.

They watched the soldiers march by solemnly, holding flags high over their heads. Then came the traditional dancers, slowly, in buckskin and feathers, porcupine quills, shells, beads—all things from nature. The fancy dancers followed in a burst of twirling bright colors. Next came the bouncing jingle dancers, their dresses covered with cones of silver and gold.

The many dancers snaked through the arena in a parade of color and magic. All wore their treasured eagle feathers with special pride.

Lorraine's eyes were on the powwow princess. Her shiny black hair was pulled back in tight rows of braids and beadwork, and her fringed dance shawl sparkled in the sunlight.

"If I were the powwow princess," Lorraine boasted, "my shawl would glitter like gold. When I danced, people would admire my steps. I would win every contest."

Raymond watched the head boy dancer arch his feathered back like a mountain lion. "If I was the head dancer boy," he said, "I would dance just for you, Rainy." He smiled shyly and pulled his big T-shirt over his knees.

Raymond ran out for the first dance. Lorraine felt a deep sadness. Her brother was still young enough to dance any way he liked, but she had come of an age to choose a style of dance and to be given a special name.

Her heart ached as she looked around and saw families dancing together. She saw a young father dressed in neon-colored feathers, holding his baby son in his arms. A miniature headdress bobbed over the little boy's eyes. She saw three sisters, all in jingle dresses. Two of the sisters were younger than Lorraine. Was she already too old to choose a dance?

Lorraine didn't come from a powwow family. She had no uncle to give her an eagle feather. She had no other relatives who could help her learn to dance.

Lorraine frowned. "They will call me Chicken Feathers!" she said angrily.

Lorraine ran from the dance arbor and wandered through the village of sturdy tipis, spread like the white tailfeathers of eagles against the blue sky.

At the edge of the tipis, Lorraine sulked under the cool pines. She sat on a carpet of shiny green plants called Kinnikinnick, a favorite herb of the older people. The throbbing drumbeats from the arbor soothed Lorraine and reminded her that she had a path to follow. She plucked the small, healing plants and gathered them in her skirt. Then she went back to the old woman with her handful of herbs, remembering that among native people, the honor is to give.

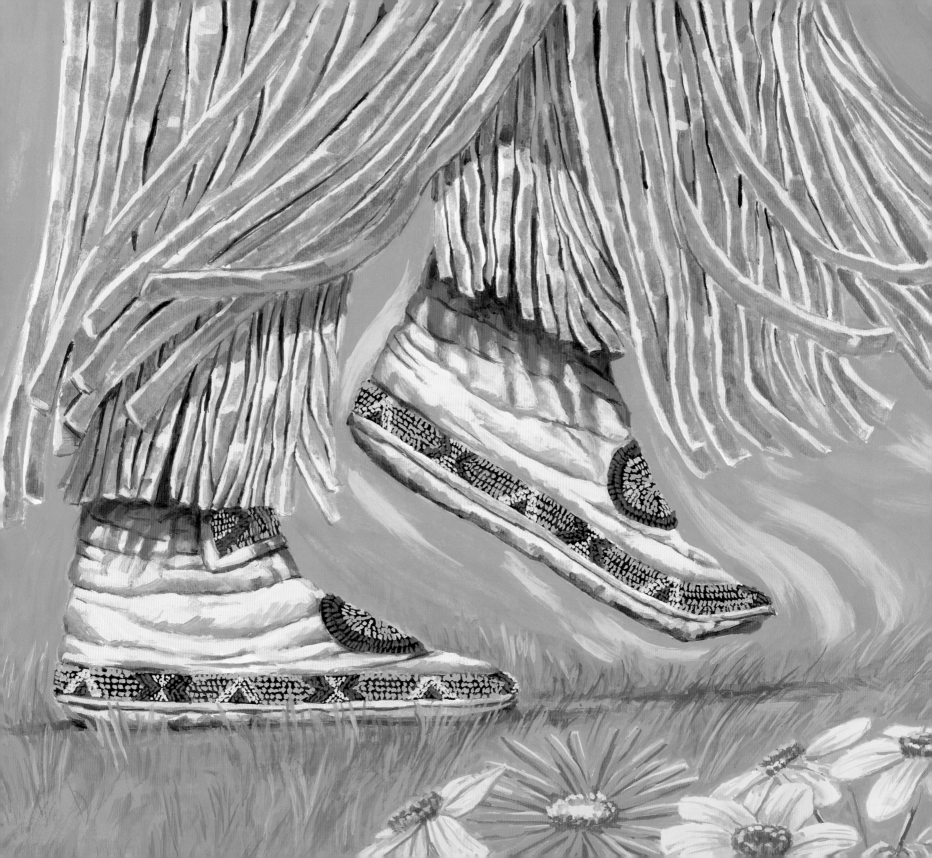

"Grandmother," she said earnestly, shaking hands gently, respectfully, in the way of her tribe. "You have lived a long time. What can you tell me of the traditional dancers?"

Grandmother White Hair seemed pleased. Her eyes looked to a long ago place. "When I dance," she said, "I am filled with reverence for Mother Earth. I walk slowly, with great respect. My moccasins touch the ground so tenderly, *touch-step, touch-step*. I carry the fan of sacred eagle feathers like a living being and offer my prayers for all the world."

Lorraine tried to imagine herself in the picture Grandmother's words painted. But she was a girl who liked to run, not walk! Still, the drum beats had spoken to her under the pine trees, in a peaceful place of nature. Was she a traditional dancer?

Lorraine thanked Grandmother and went to find the powwow princess, who was closer to her age.

Saleen, the powwow princess, was a fancy shawl dancer who had won many contests. She smoothed and fixed her braids for the next song.

"I feel like a bird with jeweled wings when I dance," she said. "I feel free to move and fly wherever the drums take me." Then she was heading out into the arena.

"Yes, surely this twirling, flying dance is for a girl like me," Lorraine thought. She watched Saleen, but the steps seemed much quicker than Lorraine's eyes could take in. The very wildness of it made her wonder if she should find something a little closer to the ground.

Lorraine thought of her friend Celeste, who was a jingle dancer. She saw Celeste's round face in the crowd, went to her and asked, "What can you tell me of the jingle dancers, Celeste?"

"When I dance," Celeste said, smiling, "I feel like music. My silver cones bounce and jingle with the drum beats, a tinkling sound that joins with all the other jingle dancers. I turn—this way, that way—but not too much. Sometimes I hold my eagle feathers tucked close to my side, like a bird at rest. And sometimes I lift them high and salute the mighty drum."

Celeste hugged her. "Rainy, the singers are singing a song for all the tribes now." She wrapped Lorraine in a shawl and playfully tugged her out into the dance circle. "It's time to powwow!"

Lorraine felt smooth, hard dirt under her feet as she moved slowly into the arena. She looked around and saw dancers of every kind stream onto the dance grounds. She heard the music of jingle dresses, *tch-tch-tch*, like raindrops on a tin roof. Out of the corner of her eye she saw the blur of a fancy shawl dancer. Grass dancers, men wearing colorful yarn costumes, moved with the drum beats, their ankle bells ringing.

They looked like birds hunting prey in the grass, teetering on silent tip-toes, barely catching themselves before swooping down. Best of all, little children danced their own dances.

Lorraine realized she wasn't moving. She was like a polished rock in the middle of a river, and the river moved smoothly around her.

She listened to the drumbeats with all her heart. They seemed to her like the earth's own heartbeat. Looking up, she saw the eagle circling as if with the stream of dancers. Slowly, at first, her feet made shy, tender steps upon the ground. The singing so filled her that it seemed a part of herself. With her arms outstretched, she felt the air move over her shawl like wings.

Then the music stopped, abruptly, with a final drum beat. Lorraine kept dancing until the sound of laughter reached her. She felt heat come to her face. Everyone had stopped dancing. They were looking at her and laughing.

Lorraine ran crying from the dance arbor. When she looked up, she saw Grandmother White Hair, bent over her cane, and little Raymond beside her.

"Rainy," said Raymond softly, touching a tear with his small fingers. He took his sister's hand.

"I feel so ashamed," she said. "I will never learn to dance!"

Grandmother smiled warmly. "Granddaughter, when we are born, do we come into the world full-grown and talking and walking?"

Lorraine smiled a little. "Of course not."

"That's right," Grandmother said. "We wave our arms and kick our legs. Then we crawl and take our first clumsy steps. That is the dance of babies."

She looked deep into Lorraine's eyes. "Was the Creator pleased with your dance, Granddaughter?" the old woman asked kindly.

Lorraine remembered how her feet touched gently upon Mother Earth, with reverence, how her mind felt filled with music, and how with wings outstretched, she flew with the eagle to the heartbeat of the earth. As she danced, she did not think about a contest, or how she looked, but only of the dance.

"Yes," she said with confidence. "I know the Creator was pleased with my dance."

"Now that you have taken your first baby-steps, you will be given the dance of your girlhood," Grandmother said.

While they spoke, a quiet had fallen over the gathering. The drums were silent. Lorraine could see a solemn group of elders gathered in a close knot in the arena. They were staring at something on the ground.

"An eagle feather has dropped to the ground. That is a bad thing," said one of the elders.

"No, I saw it fall from the sky. It is a blessing!" said another.

All of a sudden, Lorraine's friend Celeste came running toward her. People were looking at Lorraine again, but this time they were not laughing.

"Rainy!" Celeste called, her jingle dress bouncing and clattering loudly. She arrived out of breath. A slow drumbeat filled the air. "Saleen wants to have a special dance for you. Everyone at the gathering will join hearts and welcome you into the powwow family. Come!"

In the arena, Saleen approached Lorraine and held out a beautiful soft feather, a plume. "Little sister," Saleen said. "An eagle circled the arbor during the dance and dropped this in your path. In this way, the eagle has honored you with a name. White Plume Dancing, this is your eagle feather."

Rays of golden, afternoon sunlight shimmered through the dance arbor as the dance began. Lorraine felt many eyes on her as she took her first stiff, awkward steps. She stroked the sleek eagle plume in her hand, wishing for the steps that would be the dance of her girlhood.

Looking up, Lorraine saw Grandmother sitting alone under the arbor, her eyes closed as if she were sleeping. But she was not asleep. Her feet were moving ever so tenderly on the hard dirt, *touch-step, touch-step.* Suddenly, Grandmother's eyes popped open, and she was looking directly at Lorraine. Her eyes seemed to ask a question.

Lorraine thought of the things she had learned from Grandmother, Saleen, and Celeste. She thought of each dance in turn, as if holding each in her hands. Then she looked at little Raymond beside her, smiling his missing-tooth smile. She had learned something from him, too. He had dreamed of dancing just for her. She had almost missed the most important lesson of all.

Lorraine smiled back at Grandmother White Hair. She touched her feet gently upon the ground in the way of the traditional dancer, *touch-step, touch-step.* "Yes, Grandmother, I will dance for you," she said with her eyes. "I will take your place in the powwow circle."

For that is the way it is among her people—the honor is to give.

# Glossary of Powwow Terms and Dances

*There are hundreds of different tribes among the native people of North America. For these descendants of the first Americans, the powwow is a special event that gathers together modern Indians of different tribes, all with languages and customs as foreign to each other as to non-Indians. So, over the years, the powwow has come to have a language all its own, with certain agreed-upon styles of dance and regalia.*

**Arbor, Arena:** An arbor is a circular, outdoor structure with shaded areas for seating. Sometimes, as in this story, arbor refers to the shaded areas and arena to the uncovered dance area in the center. Powwows can take place anywhere, often in school gyms.

**Drum:** Both the instrument and the group of singers gathered around it are called "the drum." The main group of singers in the center of the arena is called the "host drum." It is sometimes said that the drum symbolizes the earth's heartbeat.

*The Drum*

**Eagle Feather:** The most valuable part of a dancer's outfit is the eagle feather. It can be as simple as a small plume in a girl's hair, a fan, or an entire bustle (circular, winglike arrangement) worn on the back of some male dancers. The feathers are cared for as living beings—washed, preened, and treated with utmost respect.

In modern times, eagle feathers are obtained from federal wildlife officials who have authority over these endangered birds even when found dead. Powwow dancers receive their feathers from family members or other dancers who stand in the place of relatives.

*Eagle Feather*

**Fan:** Eagle or other feathers arranged in the shape of a fan, bound at the base with leather, beadwork, or other adornments. Dancers raise their fans and salute the drum on strong downbeats.

*Fancy Dancer*

### Fancy-shawl Dancer, Fancy Dancer:

In the girl's category, graceful, twirling dance steps are performed while holding onto decorated, fringed shawls. A boy fancy dancer is a blur of bright colors. He wears a spiked hairpiece called a "roach" on his head and two feather bustles at the waist and shoulders.

**Grand Entry:** At the start of each powwow session, the dancers, or just those competing in the contests, will line up in a certain order to enter the dance arena. Usually the parade is led by the flag bearers—those who have served in the U.S. military, followed by the elders and royalty, and then the traditional, fancy, grass, and jingle-dress dancers. Sometimes the small children bring up the tail of this colorful event.

**Grass Dancer:** Usually a young man's category, these dancers make quite a spectacle with their unique and animated dance moves and colorful yarn fringes flying. A beaded headband and roach are worn on the head, but no bustles.

*Grass Dancer*

**Head Boy Dancer:** Experienced dancers are often given titles and positions to honor their dedication or success. For example, there is an arena director, a head man and woman dancer, and a head boy and girl dancer. These honored dancers may receive a modest payment for their presence. In this story, little Raymond calls the head boy dancer a "head dancer boy."

**Intertribal:** When Rainy is pulled out to dance to a "song for all the tribes," the announcer or emcee has probably just called out "Intertribal!" When this call is heard, dancers know that everyone is welcome to come out onto the floor and dance, no matter what their style of dance or experience.

### Jingle-dress Dancer, Jingle Dancer:

A popular women's or girl's category, these dancers wear dresses that are covered with rows of metal cones. The dancers must learn to bounce gracefully— with one hand on the hip and the other holding a fan—so that the cones jingle with a pleasing sound, rather than clatter. The cones are now made from the tin lids of chewing tobacco cans. The story often told of the first jingle-dress is that it was made by an Ojibwa medicine man in order to save the life of his daughter. It was covered with shells—one for every day of the year.

*Jingle-dress Dancer*

**Powwow:** Sometimes called a fair or gathering, powwows are popular throughout the United States and Canada—not only among Native Americans but among the many non-Indians who have come to enjoy them as well. Besides the contest categories described in this book, there are often social dances, games, and "giveaways" in which presents are given away by particular dancers who wish to honor those who have helped or inspired them. In Rainy's story, she and her parents would most likely have a giveaway honoring Grandmother White Hair, Saleen, Celeste, the singers, and even her little brother, Raymond.

The word "powwow" was first used in English by the governor of Plymouth Colony in 1624, but it is possible that it came from the earlier French explorers who misunderstood a native word.

*Traditional Dancer*

**Powwow Princess:** One of the most beautiful sights at a powwow is the royalty—poised girls and women wearing their winning outfits and satin sashes bearing their titles from this or other powwows.

*Fancy-shawl Dancer*

**Special:** A dance held to honor an individual or family, or to assist someone in need, is sometimes referred to as a "special."

**Traditional Dancer:** It is said that all powwow dances are just variations of the traditional style. These dancers create their outfits from nature—fur, buckskin, quills, shells—and materials that were available from the early Europeans, such as beads, cotton, trade cloth, and ribbon.

Women and girls walk very nobly, each carrying a shawl over one arm, the fringe swaying gracefully back and forth. A fan is carried in the other hand. Men and boys may imitate hunters, warriors, or certain animals in their movements and dress.